Preacher's Night Before Christmas

Preacher's Night Before Christmas

By Steven L. Layne

Illustrated by Carol Benioff

PELICAN PUBLISHING COMPANY

GRETNA 2006

Text copyright © 2006
By Steven L. Layne

Illustrations copyright © 2006
By Carol Benioff

The word "Pelican" and the depiction of a pelican are trademarks of Pelican Publishing Company, Inc., and are registered in the U.S. Patent and Trademark Office.

Library of Congress Cataloging-in-Publication Data

Layne, Steven L.
  Preacher's night before Christmas / by Steven L. Layne ; illustrated by Carol Benioff.
    p. cm.
  Summary: Everything is going wrong as Pastor McDougall tries to get ready for the Christmas Eve play, and it takes a visit from St. Nick to remind him what Christmas is really about.
  ISBN-13: 978-1-58980-321-3 (hardcover : alk. paper)
  1. Priests—Juvenile poetry. 2. Santa Claus—Juvenile poetry.
3. Christmas—Juvenile poetry. 4. Children's poetry, American.
[1. Santa Claus—Poetry. 2. Christmas—Poetry. 3. American poetry.
4. Narrative poetry.]   I. Benioff, Carol, ill. II. Moore, Clement Clarke, 1779-1863. Night before Christmas. III. Title.
PS3612.A96P74 2006
811'.54—dc22

                                                        2006003334

Printed in Singapore
Published by Pelican Publishing Company, Inc.
1000 Burmaster Street, Gretna, Louisiana 70053

PREACHER'S NIGHT BEFORE CHRISTMAS

'Twas the night before Christmas
At Spring Lane Creek Church,
And Pastor McDougall
Was in quite a lurch,

For the Christmas Eve service
His church had been planning
Had hit some snafus—
For a start, *baby banning!*

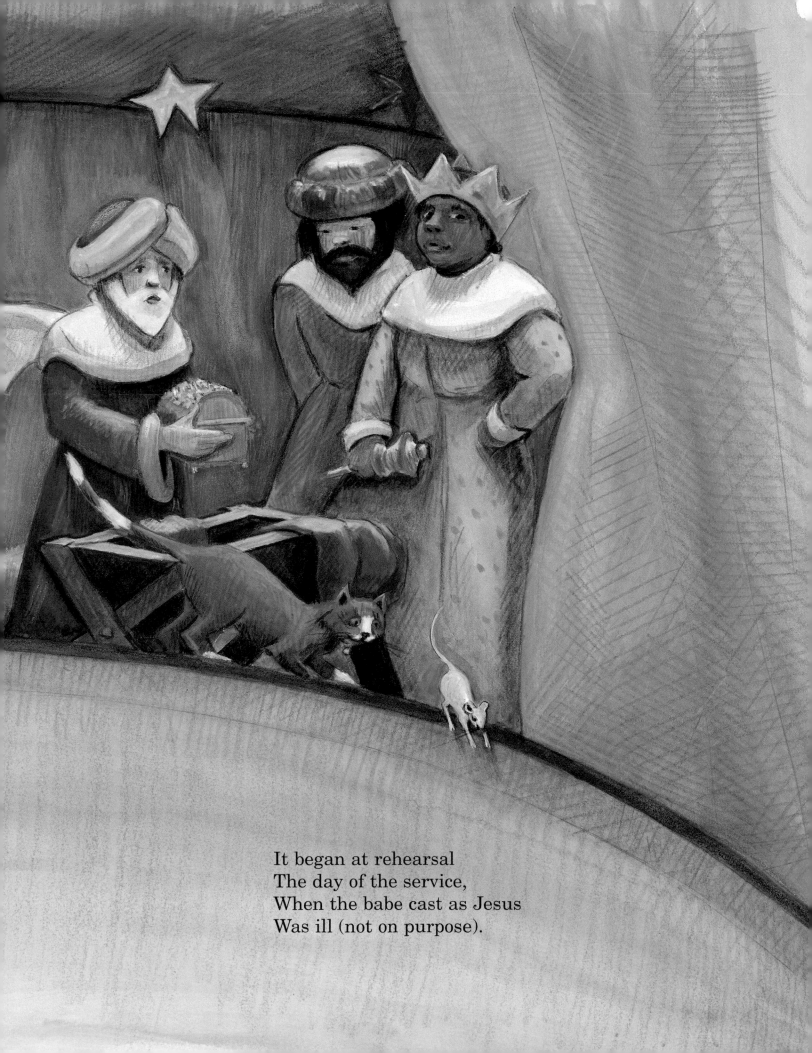

It began at rehearsal
The day of the service,
When the babe cast as Jesus
Was ill (not on purpose).

So Sally Mae Mild,
Who had such a good heart,
Rushed her Michael to church
To take over the part.

Well, Ms. Veda Ann Smith,
Who had drafted the play,
Took one long look at Michael
And said, "There's no way!"

"Oh, his ears are too large,
And his nose isn't cute;
Mike's just *not* what we're
looking for, Sally. Now scoot!"

Veda found a great flaw
To point out in each child.
Soon the kids were *all* gone,
And then Veda went wild.

But Pastor could not solve her problems—
Not yet—
'Cause the choir needed help;
They were *really* upset,

For the singers all wanted
To wear festive clothes,
But Tim Tins, their director,
Assigned them black robes.

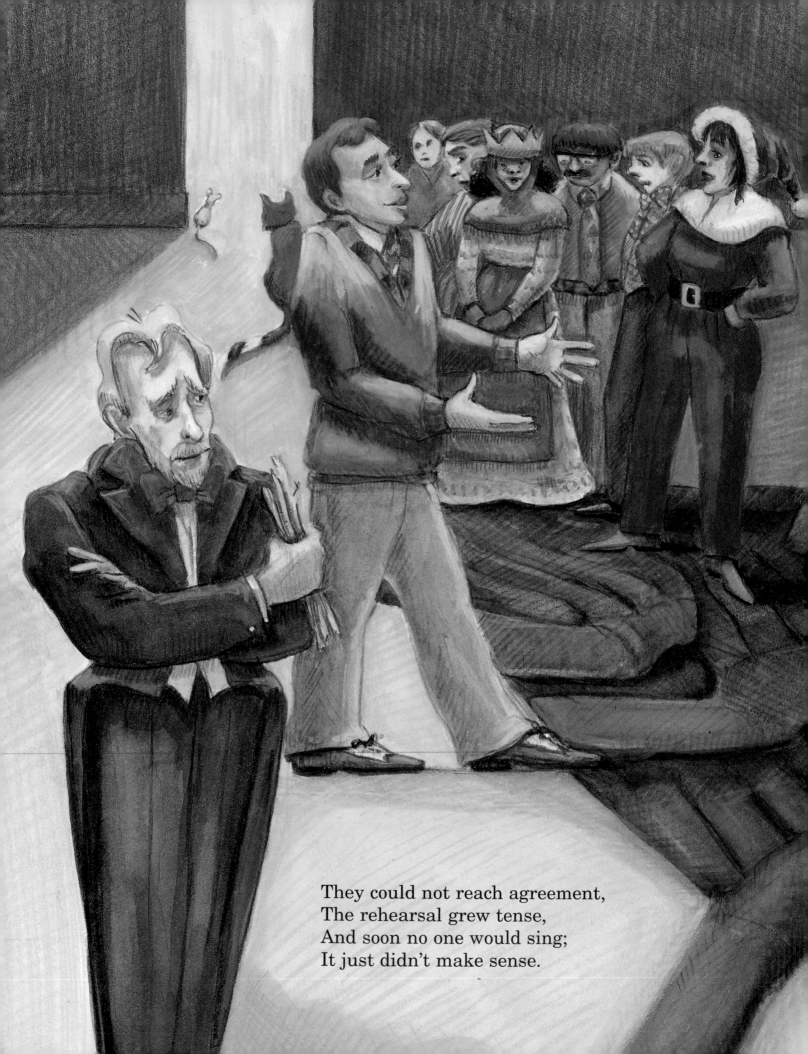

They could not reach agreement,
The rehearsal grew tense,
And soon no one would sing;
It just didn't make sense.

Pastor tried to negotiate
Some sort of peace,
But before he could do so,
They all heard loud shrieks.

Volunteers in the workroom
Had become downright mean
(They'd been fighting all day
With the copy machine).

"Well, how *can* we print programs?"
Shouted Ray, Tom, and Sue,
"With defective equipment,
This will just never do!

"We've wasted all day,
And the programs aren't done.
Let's just quit and go home;
This has stopped being fun."

But before the good pastor
Could settle *that* mess,
The church secretary
Rushed in looking stressed.

"Pastor! Oh, Pastor!
You had better come quick;
There's a man in your office
Who insists he's St. Nick!

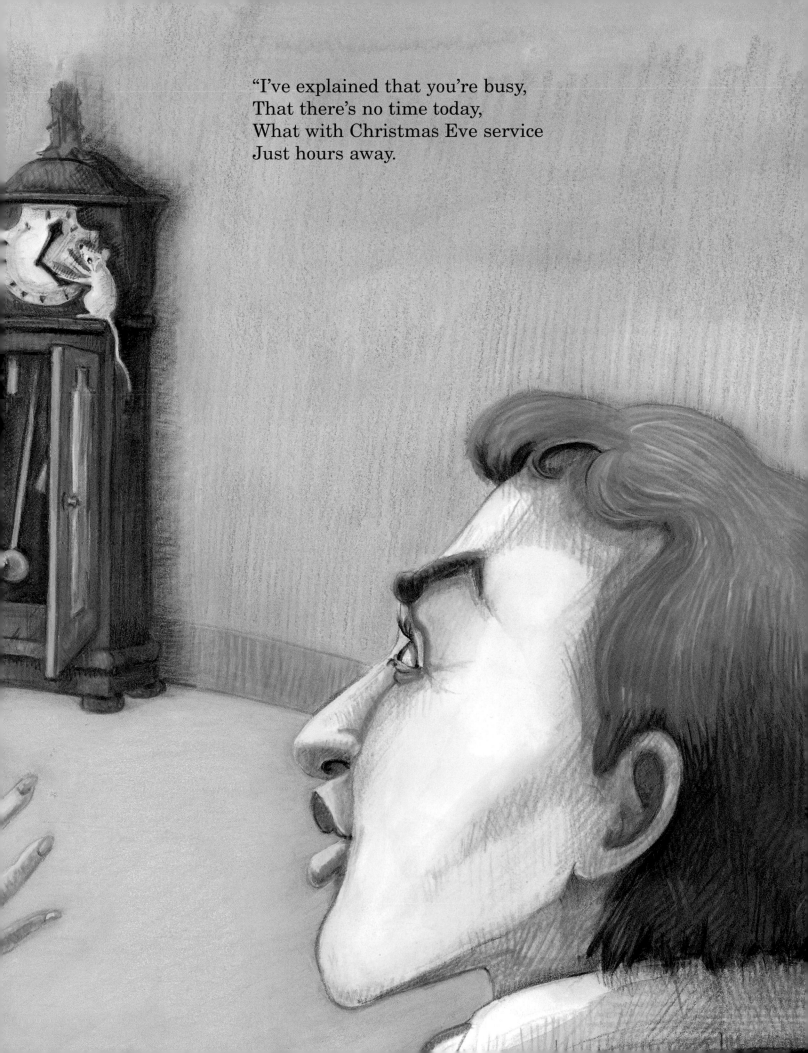

"I've explained that you're busy,
That there's no time today,
What with Christmas Eve service
Just hours away.

"But, sir, he won't leave;
I don't know what to do.
He says we need help,
And so, *I need you!*"

The pastor dashed off,
His thoughts raced without pause:
How could *he* "unbefuddle"
A confused Santa Claus?

Pastor entered his office,
The door gently closed,
And the man in the red suit said,
"Now just suppose . . .

"That you open the Good Book
And select a few pages
To remind them this night
Tells a tale for the ages."

As the pastor was reading,
A smile warmed his face;
He then looked back to Santa,
But there wasn't a trace.

Pastor rushed to the stage
With a message to share,
But his flock was all smiling;
He could not help but stare.

"*Santa* stopped by,"
Veda said with a tear,
"For he'd noticed we'd lost
All our holiday cheer."

"Even worse," said Tim Tins,
"We'd lost sight of the reason
We all should rejoice
In this glorious season."

"But how can it be?"
Pastor asked, "Is it true?
While we met in my office,
He was *also* with you?"

Then, in silent response,
A pure heavenly light
Lit the Christ child's small manger
Like a star shining bright.

And they heard sleigh bells jingle
While a voice cried with might,
"Merry Christmas to all
On this miracle night!"